MALORIE

Malorie Blackman has shot to fame since she published her first book in 1990. Many prizes have come her way including the WHSmith Mind Boggling Award for HACKER, the Children's Book Award for her brilliant novel NOUGHTS AND CROSSES, and has been shortlisted for the Carnegie Prize. Several of Malorie's books have been very successfully televised.

A former computer database manager, Malorie lives in South London with her husband and daughter, and plays music in her spare time.

MALORIE BLACKMAN

Illustrated by Juliet Percival

Barn Owl Books

Meet Betsey Biggalow

– a lively young lady
who knows her own mind!

and . . .

. . . her family
Mam
Dad
Gran'ma Liz
Sherena
(Betsey's sister)
Desmond
(Betsey's brother)
Uncle George
. . . and friends
May
Prince
(Betsey's dog)
Josh

For Neil and Lizzy, with love

BARN OWL BOOKS
157 Fortis Green Road, London, N10 3LX

This selection and arrangement
published by Barn Owl Books, 2007
157 Fortis Green Road, London, N10 3LX

Distributed by Frances Lincoln,
4 Torriano Mews, Torriano Avenue, London, NW5 2RZ

Stories first published in the following books:
Betsey Biggalow is here! - 1992
Betsey Biggalow The Detective - 1992
Hurricane Betsey - 1993
Magic Betsey - 1994
Betsey's Birthday Surprise - 1996

ISBN 978 1903015 69 8

Front cover photography (girl) © Hola Images/Getty
Front cover photography (background) © Tony Hamer
Designed and typeset by Skandesign Limited
Produced in Poland by Polskabook

Contents

The Special, Special Trainers

Betsey peered in through the shoe shop window. There they were! Her special trainers. Her magic trainers. With those trainers she wouldn't just run, she'd *fly*! No one would be able to catch her in those extra special, *special* trainers.

'Betsey, come away from that window.' Gran'ma Liz frowned.

'Oh Gran'ma Liz. Look! The trainers I was telling you about – they're still there!' Betsey pointed.

'They're going to stay there too!' Gran'ma Liz said. 'Come on.'

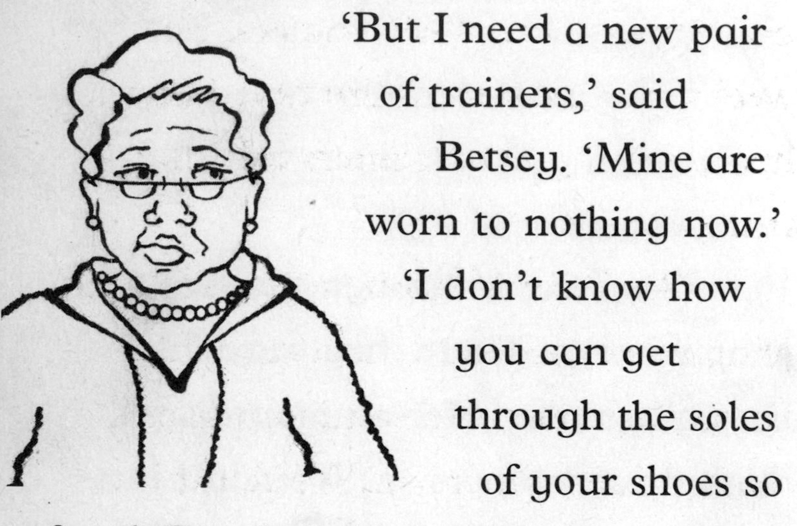

'But I need a new pair of trainers,' said Betsey. 'Mine are worn to nothing now.'

'I don't know how you can get through the soles of your shoes so fast.' Gran'ma Liz tutted. 'You must be eating them!'

'Gran'ma Liz, just look at the

trainers. Look at the colours. Look at the laces. Look at the ...'

'Look at the time!' Gran'ma Liz glanced down at her watch. 'Come on Betsey, or we'll miss our bus.'

'But Gran'ma Liz ...'

'Betsey, for the last time, I'm not buying you those trainers. For weeks now all your mam and I have heard from you is trainers this and trainers that!'

'But Gran'ma Liz, my best friend May has a pair of those trainers,' Betsey said eagerly, 'and you should see her when she runs. She doesn't run, she soars and swoops – just like a bird or a plane.'

'Betsey, you talk some real

nonsense sometimes,' said Gran'ma Liz. 'Come on, child.'

So Betsey had to leave the front of the shoe shop. She crossed her fingers tight, tight, tight.

'I want those trainers something fierce,' Betsey muttered to herself.

'What did you say, Betsey?' asked Gran'ma Liz.

'Nothing, Gran'ma,' said Betsey.

'Hhmm!' said Gran'ma. 'Hhmm!' And without another word, off they went home.

But on the way home, Betsey had an idea...

At dinner time, the family sat around the table, Gran'ma Liz and Betsey and Sherena, Betsey's bigger sister and Desmond, Betsey's bigger brother. For dinner there was cou-cou and flying fish and salad and a huge jug of delicious soursop drink mixed with milk and plenty of ice. Betsey licked her lips. Scrumptious!

'Pass the salt please, Betsey,' said Sherena.

Betsey picked up the glass salt shaker. 'The tops of the trainers I want are just as white as this salt,' said Betsey.

She pointed to the pepper bottle.

'And the soles of the trainers I want are blacker than the writing on the pepper bottle.' Sherena and Desmond looked at each other.

'Betsey, I want to hear no more about those trainers. D'you hear?'

frowned Gran'ma Liz.

'Yes, Gran'ma,' Betsey said. Betsey poured herself a glass of soursop drink, but some spilt onto the sky-blue tablecloth. The white liquid spread out.

'Betsey!' said Gran'ma Liz. 'Look at that mess.'

'That stain is just about the size of the trainers I want,' Betsey murmured.

Gran'ma Liz could stand it no longer.

'Elizabeth Ruby Biggalow, all day, all week, all *month*, you've done nothing but mope and whine about those trainers,' frowned Gran'ma Liz. 'You're long face is spoiling my day as well as my dinner. Now not another word.'

And Betsey knew that she'd better shut up. Whenever Gran'ma Liz called her by her whole, full name, Betsey knew she was treading dangerously close to trouble.

But for the rest of the evening all Betsey had in her head were her special trainers on her feet.

The next morning, when Betsey went down for breakfast, everyone was unusually quiet.

'What's the matter?' asked Betsey.

'I've got something for you.' Mam smiled, 'As your old trainers are in such a state I decided to get you some new ones.'

'You bought the trainers!' Betsey couldn't believe it.

'Now perhaps we can all get some peace,' Gran'ma Liz sniffed.

Betsey grinned and grinned. Her extra special trainers. She'd got them at last. Mam handed over the bag she was hiding behind her back. Betsey opened the bag and...

'What's the matter?' asked Sherena.

'Oh!' Betsey couldn't say anything else. Her eyes started stinging and there was a huge, choking lump in her throat.

Botheration! These weren't the ones with the white fronts and the black soles and the red laces? Where were her special trainers? Still in the shop – that's where!

These ones were pink and grey and didn't have any black writing on them like the ones she wanted.

'Betsey...' Gran'ma Liz warned. 'Your mam had to take time off work to buy those for you.'

'Don't you like them, Betsey?' Mam asked.

'They're lovely,' Betsey whispered.

'Put them on then,' urged Desmond.

Betsey sat down and, oh

so slowly she put on her new shoes.

'They look boss!' smiled Sherena.

'The best trainers I've ever seen,' said Desmond.

Gran'ma Liz didn't say anything. She just watched Betsey.

'Can I go and show them to my friend May please?' Betsey asked Mam.

'Go ahead then,' she smiled. 'But don't stay with her too long. You've still got your morning chores to finish.'

Betsey ran out of the kitchen. She couldn't wait to get out of the house. She looked at her feet. These weren't her special trainers. These shoes were just horrible. Betsey ran all the way to May's house – sprinting as if to sprint the trainers right off her feet. At May's house, Betsey knocked and knocked again. May opened the door. Worse still, May opened the door wearing the very same trainers that Betsey wanted so much.

'Hi May,' Betsey said glumly.

'Hi Betsey,' said May. 'I was just going to the beach. Coming?'

Betsey shrugged. 'Just for a little while.'

So off they went. But things weren't right. No, they weren't. By the time Betsey and May reached the beach they were having a full blown, full grown argument.

'Well, my trainers are the best in the country,' said May.

'My trainers are the best in the world,' Betsey fumed.

'Talk sense! My trainers are the best in the universe,' said May.

'I hate you and your trainers,' Betsey shouted. 'And I hate these ones I'm wearing and I hate *everything*.'

'And I hate you and your smelly shoes too,' May stormed.

Betsey and May stared and glared and scowled and glowered at each other.

Then Betsey started to smile, then to laugh, then to hold her stomach she was laughing so much.

'What's so funny?' May asked, still annoyed.

'Botheration! Imagine hating a pair of shoes!' Betsey laughed. 'You hate my shoes and I hate your shoes. And both pairs of shoes are probably laughing at us for being so foolish.'

'All this fuss over a pair of trainers,' May agreed with a giggle.

'Come on! Let's have a run. Things are always better after a run on the beach,' said Betsey. 'I'll race you to that palm tree yonder.'

'Ready ... Set ... Go ...'

And off they both sprinted, faster than fast. They leapt over the sand and through lapping water, kicking up the spray as they went, laughing and

laughing.
Until finally
they both collapsed in
the shade of the palm tree Betsey
had pointed to. Who won the race?
Neither Betsey or May cared.

Betsey glanced down at her wet
shoes. They were all right! Not the
ones she'd wanted, but a present from

her mam just the same. A special present. A wonderful surprise.

'Look at that!' said May, surprised. May pointed to her trainers. The red colour in her laces was running down the white front of her trainers and over the black writing. May's trainers didn't like getting wet – not one little bit.

Betsey glanced down at her own trainers – still grey and pink and no running colours anywhere. She jumped up.

'May, let's walk along the beach for a bit longer,' said Betsey. 'We can collect shells and paddle. Never mind our trainers. Let's walk in our bare feet.'

'Yeah! It's much nicer walking on the sand in bare feet anyway,' May agreed.

And May and Betsey ran over the white sand and through the blue

water, their trainers knotted at the
laces and dangling around their necks.

2

Betsey's Birthday Surprise

The moment Betsey opened her eyes, she expected wonderful, sun-shiny, brilliant surprises. Well, she got a surprise all right! A nasty surprise. A *horrible* surprise. Everyone had forgotten her birthday!

At first Betsey couldn't believe it.

Botheration! How could everyone have forgotten that today was her birthday?

'Gran'ma Liz, guess what today is?' Betsey asked hopefully.

'Saturday,' said Gran'ma Liz. 'Now run along and play, Betsey. I've got things to do.'

Betsey decided to give Gran'ma Liz a teeny-tiny clue.

'Gran'ma, haven't you forgotten something?' Betsey asked. 'Something wonderful about the day and *me*.'

If Gran'ma Liz didn't get it from that then she didn't deserve to call her gran'ma!

'Betsey child, what are you talking about? It's Saturday. That's it! End of story! And...' Gran'ma Liz slapped her hand against her forehead. 'I'd forget my head if it wasn't glued to my neck! Thanks for reminding me Betsey. I promised your mam I'd make some of her favourite biscuits for when she comes home from work. I'd better get started.'

'But ... but ...' That's not what Betsey meant at all!

'D'you want to help me? asked Gran'ma Liz.

No way! Not today of all days. It looked like Gran'ma Liz really *had* forgotten. Betsey wandered out into the backyard. Sherena bowled a cricket ball to Desmond who hit it into the dirt.

'Why the glum face, Betsey?'

asked Sherena as she picked up the ball.

'Because today is... today is...'

'A kind of nothing day,' Sherena finished Betsey's sentence. 'I know exactly what you mean. There's nothing to do. And it's the kind of day when you don't want to do anything either.'

Betsey really couldn't believe it.

All week she'd reminded everyone that it was her birthday on Saturday and they'd still forgotten. How *could* they? Even May hadn't sent a card. Betsey felt tears prick at her eyes.

'Sherena I can't practise hitting the ball if you don't throw it to me,' Desmond called out from the other end of the back yard.

'D'you want to stay and play cricket with us?' Sherena asked Betsey. 'You can be the wicket keeper if you like.'

'Stuff the wicket keeper!' Betsey snapped.

'Charming!' Sherena raised her eyebrows as Betsey flounced back into the house.

So it was true. They had all forgotten. Maybe Mam hadn't – but she wasn't here. But the rest had! There were no cards, no presents. And forget about a birthday cake! There wasn't even a birthday sandwich! Betsey would've settled for a birthday biscuit!

'Then I'll just have to do

something on my own!' Betsey muttered.

Yeah! That's what she'd do. She'd celebrate her own birthday – all by herself. She'd show them all. She needed to do something fun to cheer herself up. Something *different*!

'I know!' Betsey clapped her hands.

She marched into Mam and Dad's bedroom. She switched on Mam's radio to listen to some dance music. That would cheer her up for a start. Then Betsey sat at the dressing-table and picked up Mam's most expensive bottle of perfume. Dad had bought it for her especially the last time he came home.

'I have to smell nice on my birthday,' Betsey mumbled. And she squirted some on her wrists... and her neck ... and her feet and her legs ... and her arms ... and reached around to squirt some up and down her back. That was more like it! Betsey looked over the dressing-table. What next? Make-up! That would make her look better – more like a birthday girl.

'I have to look good on my birthday,' Betsey decided.

Very carefully, Betsey put on some of Mam's lipstick. Next she tried some of Mam's eye-shadow. She wasn't sure about the eye-shadow but she left it on.

What now? Betsey spotted the

very thing. She opened Mam's jewellery box and put on a pair of Mam's long, dangly earrings and her matching long, dangly necklace.

'I have to sparkle on my birthday!' Betsey smiled at herself in the dressing-table mirror.

'Clothes!' Betsey announced. 'That's what I need!'

She definitely needed some birthday clothes. She opened Mam and Dad's wardrobe. She saw the very thing. Mam's favourite black dress. Betsey pulled it off the hanger. She slipped off her own clothes and put on Mam's dress. It only reached to Mam's knees when she wore it but on Betsey it trailed onto the floor. It didn't look *too* bad though.

'Perfect! Now I really do look like a birthday girl,' Betsey said, admiring herself in the mirror. 'I think I'd better turn of the radio. I don't want anyone to come in until I've finished.'

'Betsey, could you come here for a second?' Gran'ma Liz called out.

'Coming,' Betsey replied.

She tried to walk but tripped over the bottom of the dress. Betsey lifted up the hem and tried again. That was better! She opened the bedroom door and stepped out into the living-room.

'Gran'ma Liz, how do I loo ..?' Betsey's voice trailed off slowly.

'HAPPY BIRTHDAY, BETS ...'

The living-room was full to overflowing with Betsey's friends and their parents. May was there – and Josh and Celine and Martin. Everyone was there. They'd all started to wish Betsey a happy birthday, but when they saw what she was wearing, their voices trailed off.

Betsey's voice had trailed off too. She stared and stared, wondering where all these people had suddenly come from.

'Elizabeth Ruby Biggalow, I... I...' For once Gran'ma Liz was lost for words!

One or two people started to titter. And three or four people started to giggle. Then the whole room erupted with laughter.

'Betsey, who told you to put on my best dress? And what on earth is that smell?' Mam choked. 'Child, you smell like a perfume factory.' And Mam marched Betsey into the bathroom.

'Why are all my friends here?' Betsey asked, amazed.

'Because I arranged a surprise party for you,' said Mam.

'A surprise party!' Betsey's eyes gleamed. 'For me?'

'You can rejoin it when I've got all this muck off your face and when you smell human again!' said Mam.

Whilst the bath was running, Mam stripped Betsey out of her

clothes. She washed Betsey's face and scrubbed her body until Betsey's skin felt piping hot. Then Mam gave Betsey a box wrapped in glittery paper.

'Happy birthday, Betsey,' Mam smiled. 'This is from your gran'ma and your dad and me.'

Betsey tore off the paper in about two seconds flat. It was a dress. The most beautiful dress Betsey had ever seen. It was a deep blue silk, covered with tiny, delicate flowers. Betsey hugged Mam tight.

'Thanks, Mam,' she said happily.

'Now isn't that better than my

old black dress,' Mam smiled as she led the way into the living-room.

As soon as everyone saw Betsey they all started clapping. They all agreed – Betsey looked wonderful.

'Well done, Betsey,' grinned Uncle George. 'We thought we'd surprise you with a party, but you had a surprise of your own!'

'It was my birthday surprise for all of you!' Betsey winked.

'I'm only sorry I forgot my camera at home!' laughed May's mam.

'Thank goodness you *did* forget it,' sniffed Gran'ma Liz. 'Otherwise we'd never have lived it down!'

But only Betsey heard that bit!

Finders Keepers

‘It’s mine! It’s mine! I found it! Finders keepers!’ said Betsey.

Sherena, Betsey’s bigger sister, raised her head from her history homework book.

‘What have you found?’ asked Sherena.

‘This shell necklace. Isn’t it pretty?’ Betsey replied. She held it up high for her sister to see. ‘I found it here on my bed.’

‘Betsey, you know very well that necklace is mine,’ frowned Sherena.

'No I don't,' Betsey shook her head. 'It hasn't got your name on it and it was on *my* bed. So it's mine! Finders Keepers!'

'Betsey, you toad! Give that back,' ordered Sherena.

'Won't! Won't! Won't!' said Betsey.

Sherena stood up, her eyes flashing like lightning. 'Betsey, I'm warning you. Give that back.'

'Gran'ma... GRAN'MA!' Betsey yelled. And she ran out into the sitting-room with Sherena chasing after her, trying to snatch back her necklace.

'What on earth is going on?' asked Gran'ma Liz.

'Tell Betsey to give me back my necklace, before I get annoyed,' said Sherena crossly.

'It's not her necklace. It was on my bed. It's mine! Finders keepers!' said Betsey.

Gran'ma Liz frowned. 'Betsey child! You know as well as I do that necklace belongs to your sister. Give it back.'

'But Gran'ma...'

'Elizabeth Ruby Biggalow! Give it back. Don't let me have to tell you again,' said Gran'ma Liz.

There was Gran'ma Liz using Betsey's whole, full name! That meant that Betsey had better step carefully or the next step might get her into a lot of TROUBLE!

'Botheration!' Betsey muttered under her breath. Reluctantly, she handed the necklace back to Sherena.

'Hhumph!' said Sherena, before marching back to her bedroom.

Betsey wandered out into the back yard, muttering to herself. 'So it should've been mine. It didn't have Sherena's name on it ...'

Then Betsey spied a cricket ball, lying in the middle of the yard. She ran over to it and picked it up.

'I found it! It's mine! Finders Keepers!' shouted Betsey.

'What are you mumbling about?' Desmond, Betsey's bigger brother, called out from across the back yard.

'Look what I've found, Desmond,' beamed Betsey. And she held up the cricket ball for her brother to see.

Desmond frowned. 'You've found my cricket ball there because that's where I put it.'

'This cricket ball was lying there waiting for someone to find it – and that's me!' said Betsey. 'This is my cricket ball now.'

'Betsey, give me back my ball,' said Desmond.

'I won't! It doesn't have your name on it,' Betsey replied.

'Betsey, I'm warning you ...' Desmond said.

'Won't! Won't! Won't' said Betsey. 'This ball is mine.'

'Right!' And with that, Desmond started chasing Betsey all around the garden. Betsey ducked around the breadfruit tree and ran through the chickens with Desmond racing after her.

'BETSEY! COME BACK HERE!' Desmond yelled.

Betsey ran into the house, followed by her brother.

'Wait a minute!' said Gran'ma Liz. 'If you two want to chase each other then go and do it in the back yard, not in my house.

'Gran'ma Liz! Tell Betsey to give me back my ball,' Desmond said.

'It's not his ball. I found it in the back yard,' Betsey argued.

'Betsey! What has got into you today?' asked Gran'ma Liz. 'You know as well as I do that ball belongs to your brother.'

'But ...'

'No "buts"!' said Gran'ma Liz. 'Give Desmond back his ball.'

And although Betsey huffed and puffed and pouted, she had to hand over the cricket ball. Sherena came out of her bedroom just as Betsey went out into the back yard.

'What's going on?' Sherena asked.

'Betsey's playing silly games,' sniffed Desmond. 'She took my cricket ball and insisted it was hers just because I wasn't holding it at the time.'

'She did the same thing to me. She said my shell necklace was hers just because I didn't put my name on it,' said Sherena.

'I think it's time we taught Betsey Biggalow a lesson,' winked Gran'ma Liz.

So Sherena and Desmond gathered around as Gran'ma Liz told

them of her plan.

That evening, Uncle George came round for dinner. While Betsey was out of the room, Gran'ma Liz grabbed Uncle George for a quick secret chat. Then they all sat down to dinner – and what a dinner it was too! Vegetable and dumpling soup, the way only Gran'ma Liz could make it.

'Betsey, what have you been up to today?' asked Uncle George.

Betsey glanced at Sherena who was staring at her. Then Betsey glanced at Desmond, who was glaring at her.

'Er ... nothing much, Uncle George,' said Betsey, taking another spoonful of her soup.

'Betsey! What's that behind you?' Sherena suddenly called out.

Betsey quickly turned her head. 'Where? Where?'

'Over there,' said Sherena, pointing to the corner of the ceiling.

'I can't see anything,' Betsey frowned. Betsey turned back to her soup. The bowl was empty ... Betsey stared and stared, but it didn't help. Her bowl was still empty.

'Where's my soup gone?' Betsey asked, amazed.

'Oh, was it your soup?' asked Uncle George. 'I didn't know that. It was just sitting on the table, so I helped myself.'

'But ... but ... but that was *my*

soup,' Betsey spluttered.

'It didn't have your name on it, Betsey,' said Gran'ma Liz. 'So how was your uncle to know it was yours?'

'Because ... because ... the bowl was in front of me,' said Betsey.

'But the whole table is in front of me. So the table and everything on it in mine,' said Uncle George. 'Finders Keepers!'

'But that's not fair,' said Betsey.

'In fact, not only does the table and everything on it belong to me, but everyone at the table belongs to me too!' said Uncle George.

And Uncle George stood up and went over to Betsey. Before she could say "dumplings!", Uncle George picked her up and threw her over his shoulder.

'Look what I've found everyone,' grinned Uncle George. 'This girl was just sitting here and I found her. As she hasn't got anyone's name on her, I'm going to keep her. Finders keepers!'

'You can keep her for as long as you like, Uncle!' said Desmond.

'Uncle! Uncle! Put me down,' yelled Betsey.

'Who said that?' said Uncle George, looking around.

'I said it, Uncle George. Put me down,' said Betsey.

'Why?'

'Because I ... I don't belong to

you,' said Betsey.

'Who do you belong to then?' asked Uncle George.

'I belong to ... myself,' Betsey decided.

'Where does it say that?' asked Uncle George.

'It doesn't say that anywhere. But it's true,' said Betsey.

'What about this shell necklace? Whose is it?' asked Sherena, holding up the necklace for Betsey to see.

'It's yours. Mam gave it to you for your last birthday,' Betsey replied.

Desmond held up a cricket ball. 'And who does this belong to?' he asked.

'It's yours,' said Betsey. 'It's the

special one Dad bought for you.'

'So have we heard the last of this finders keepers nonsense?' asked Gran'ma Liz.

'Yes! Yes! I'm never going to say those two words ever, *ever* again,' said Betsey.

'In that case, I'll put you down,' said Uncle George. And he put Betsey back on her feet.

'And I'll give you some more soup,' smiled Gran'ma Liz.

Gran'ma Liz filled Betsey's bowl with some soup from the pot. Betsey helped herself to some more dumplings.

When Sherena finished her soup, she peered into the pot.

'Gran'ma Liz, are there any more dumplings left?' asked Sherena.

'Sorry, Sherena. Betsey had the last one,' Gran'ma Liz replied.

'Finders keepers!' said Betsey.

4

Hurricane Betsey

'Sherena, Desmond, Betsey, come in here a minute,' called Mam.

Sherena came in from the back yard where she was polishing her bike. Desmond came in from his bedroom where he was doing his homework – for once! Betsey was already in the sitting-room.

'What's the matter, Mam?' asked Sherena.

Mam looked worried.

'I've got some bad news,' said Mam at last. 'There's been a hurricane warning on the TV. Hurricane Boris is heading this way.'

'A hurricane?' asked Betsey.

'Oh, you've never seen a hurricane have you?' said Desmond, his eyes big and round like saucers.

'A hurricane is like a huge, ferocious storm with winds gusting at over one hundred and fifteen kilometres an hour. The winds are so strong, they can lift you right off your feet and they can blow down trees and blow the roofs off houses and make the sea spin with giant waves and ...'

'That's quite enough, Desmond,' said Mam sternly.

'Will we spin up and up in the air as well?' asked Betsey quickly.

'Of course not,' said Mam. 'As long as we stay in the house, we'll be fine.'

'But I *want* to spin up and up in the air,' said Betsey, very disappointed. 'I want to fly.'

'Then you'll just have to wait until you fly in an aeroplane like the rest of us,' said Sherena. 'If a hurricane spun you up in the air, when you landed you'd probably break almost every bone in your body ...'

'That's quite enough from you as well, Sherena,' frowned Mam.

'What should we do, Mam?' asked Desmond.

'I want the three of you to help me pack away all the breakable things,' said Mam.

Betsey stared and stared.

'What's the matter, Betsey?' asked Mam.

'I don't want to be packed away! I don't want to be packed away!' Betsey sniffed, very close to tears.

Everyone burst out laughing.

'Betsey, child! We're not going

to pack *you* away,' said Gran'ma Liz.

'We'd never find a box big enough!' muttered Desmond.

'We're going to pack up my best plates and glasses and anything else that's fragile,' Mam told Betsey.

'Fragile?' said Betsey.

'That means easily breakable,' Sherena told her. 'And Betsey, you *aren't* fragile!'

So that's what they did. Betsey and Sherena and Desmond wrapped up Mam's best glasses and plates and ornaments in newspaper before putting them into boxes.

'Mam, where do we go so we don't get swirled up and whirled up into the air?' asked Betsey.

'We'll stay in the sitting-room,' Mam answered.

'Will it be safe?' asked Betsey anxiously.

'Of course. We'll be together, won't we?' smiled Gran'ma Liz.

'Sherena, bring your bike in from outside, and Betsey, go and get Prince from the back yard please,' said Mam.

Prince was the family Alsatian dog.

Betsey ran out into the back yard to fetch him. Once outside, Betsey noticed that the leaves of the breadfruit tree were jiggling madly, as if dancing to some music that Betsey couldn't hear.

'A hurricane is coming! A hurricane is coming!' Betsey shouted out.

And she whirled and twirled

around, knocking the flowerpots off the ledge beside her.

'BETSEY! Bring Prince inside and stop dancing about, said Gran'ma Liz. 'Hurricanes are serious business and nothing to be glad about.'

'Yes, Gran'ma,' said Betsey.

Betsey looked up at the sky. It was dark and grey and she couldn't see the sun. A drop of water landed on

her forehead, then another drop landed on her cheek. The storm was beginning. Betsey called Prince over and together they went into the house.

'What else should I do, Mam?' asked Betsey.

'Now we have to board up all the windows so that they don't blow in on us,' said Mam, looking around. 'Sherena, Gran'ma and I will do that. You and Desmond fill all the flasks in the house with water. Then make sure that the bath tub and the sink are clean and fill them with cold water as well.'

'Why do we have to do that?' asked Betsey.

'The hurricane might disrupt the

water supply, so we want to make sure we've got enough drinking water to last us for a while,' Mam explained.

For the rest of the morning, the whole family was busy, busy, busy, but at last everything was done.

'Desmond, bring your homework in here so you can carry on with it,' said Gran'ma Liz.

'Do I have to?' Desmond pleaded.

'Yes, you do. Sherena, if you've got any homework, you might as well do it now too,' said Gran'ma Liz.

'We'll all stay in this one room and watch the TV for news of the hurricane,' said Mam.

Betsey sat next to Mam, who put

her arm around Betsey's shoulders.

'Will we be alright?' Betsey whispered.

'Of course we will,' smiled Mam.

Outside, Betsey could hear the heavy rain splashing against the roof and windows and she could hear the wind howling around the house.

'Please stay in your homes and listen to your radios or your TVs for further information. Please do not use your phone unless it is an emergency. Please stay in your homes and listen to your radios and TVs for further information.'

'What's that?' Betsey squeaked. 'Don't worry, Betsey. It's just the police, advising people about what they should do,' said Mam.

'They'll drive around for as long as they can. talking through a loudspeaker so that everyone can hear them.'

'Oh!' said Betsey, and she cuddled up closer to Mam.

A while later, an announcement came on the TV.

'This is a hurricane update. The hurricane has changed course and is now headed out to sea. Repeat. The hurricane has changed course and is now heading out to sea.'

'Thank goodness for that.' Gran'ma Liz gave a sigh of relief.

'We're still going to get stormy weather for a while but at least the hurricane won't be passing this way,' said Mam. 'Okay, everyone, let's start unpacking the boxes and putting everything back in it's place.'

Betsey sprang up off the sofa and ran to the nearest box.

'I'll help. Let me help,' she said, picking up the box which was filled with a few glasses wrapped in newspaper. Betsey whirled and twirled around with the box in her hands. 'The hurricane has gone! The hurricane has gone!' she grinned. But because of the box, Betsey didn't see that she was heading straight for Prince ...

'No, Betsey ...'

'Don't ...'

Too late. Betsey tripped over Prince and the box of glasses in her hands went flying up into the air to land with an enormous

SMAAAAASH-CRAAAAASH!

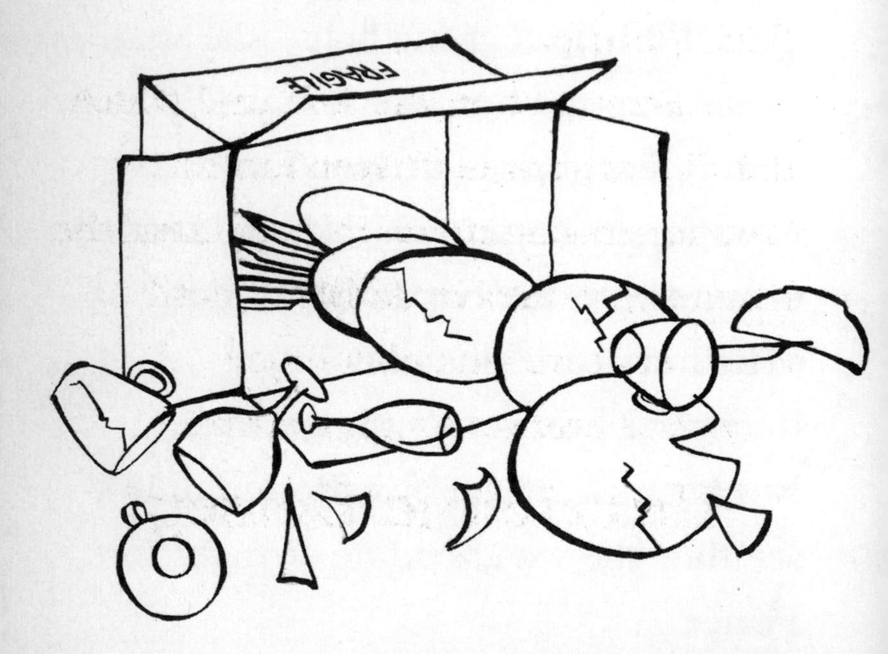

All of the glasses in the box were shattered!

'Betsey stared at the box.

'Is everyone all right? No one got cut, did they?' said Mam.

Everyone was fine – except Betsey.

'Mam, it wasn't me. It was ...' Betsey began.

'Betsey sit on the sofa and watch the TV,' interrupted Gran'ma Liz. 'You're causing more damage than the hurricane would've done! In fact I know what we should call you ...'

And everyone shouted out,

'Hurricane Betsey!'

Betsey and the Mighty Marble

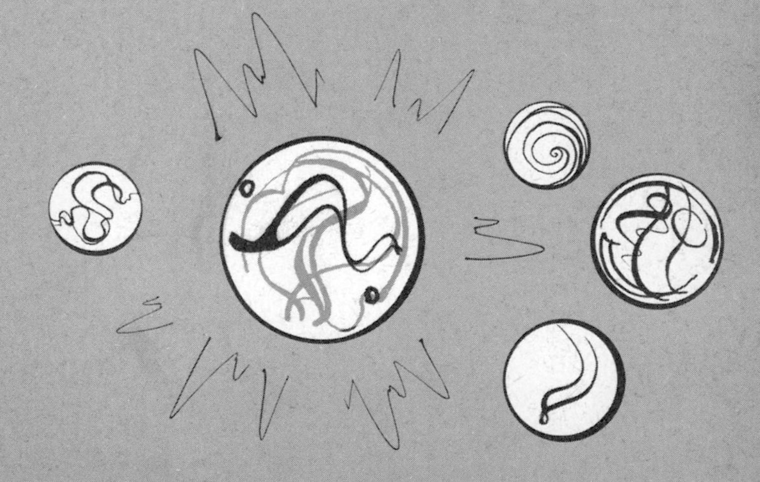

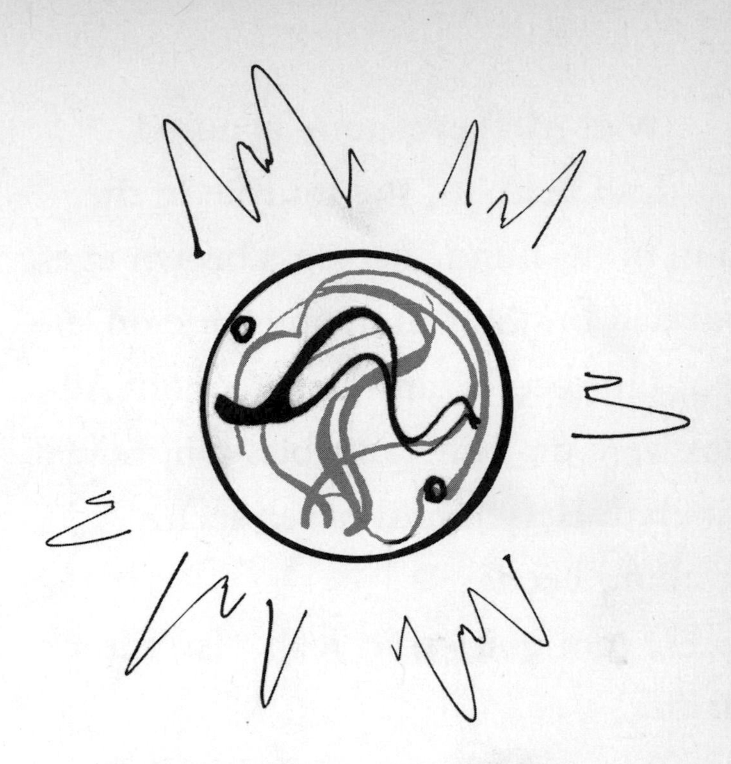

'I've got a marble. A mighty marble,' said Josh proudly. School had finished for the day and there was still plenty of afternoon left to play in. Betsey and her friends were on the beach.

'Who wants to look at the mighty marble?' Josh called out.

'Me! Me!' everyone shouted.

Josh held out the marble in the palm of his hand. Betsey's brown eyes sparkled brighter than sunshine on the clear blue sea behind her. Ooooh! All eyes were on Josh's marble. Oh, how it glittered! Betsey had never seen anything like it.

'I told you,' said Josh. 'Isn't it terrific?'

It was the biggest marble Betsey had ever seen and it was filled with sky blue and leaf green moonlight silver slivers.

'It's the most beautiful marble in the world,' Betsey breathed. And all at once, she wanted that marble. She wanted that marble something fierce.

'Josh,' began Betsey, holding up her bag of marbles. 'I'll swap you ten of my marbles for your mighty marble.'

'No way,' Josh scoffed. 'Mr Mighty Marble is staying with me!'

'I'll swap you *twenty* of my marbles for your mighty marble,' said May.

Soon the air was filled with 'I'll swap you this', and 'I'll swap you that', but Josh only laughed and

held Mr Mighty Marble up higher.

Betsey looked at the super marble in Josh's hands. It seemed to be calling out to her, teasing her.

'Betsey ...' whispered Mr Mighty Marble. 'Betsey, look at me. Aren't I just the most perfect, the most splendid marble in the world!' And what could Betsey reply but, 'You are! You are!'

Betsey dug her hand into her dress pocket and slowly took out Old Faithful.

Old Faithful was a small marble, perfect but clear, with a single gold streak like a summer lightning flash caught in its middle. Betsey's dad had given it to her.

'You look after Old Faithful,' said Dad. 'And Old Faithful will look after you.'

It was Betsey's special marble and all her friends admired it, but Betsey never played with it. Old Faithful was too small to play with.

'Josh,' said Betsey, 'let's have a contest right now. Your Mr Mighty Marble against my best marble.'

'Why should I?' frowned Josh.

''Cause if you win, I'll give you every marble I've got,' said Betsey slowly. She held up her full bag of marbles. 'You'll get every single marble in here.'

Josh's eyes gleamed. 'Including Old Faithful?'

Betsey looked at the marble her dad had given her. Next to Mr Mighty Marble, Old Faithful looked dull and titch-tiny and hardly worth bothering with at all.

'Including Old Faithful,' Betsey agreed at last.

'Betsey! You can't do that,' said May. 'You're dad gave you Old Faithful.

'May, don't worry,' said Betsey. 'If I win, I'll get Josh's super marble.'

'And what happens if you lose?' asked May, her hands on her hips.

Betsey thought about it, long and

hard. If she lost then Josh would end up with every single marble she had in the world – including Old Faithful. Dad had played marbles with Old Faithful when he was a boy and he'd given her Old Faithful as a present.

How could she give away a present from her dad? She shouldn't have told Josh she'd give him Old Faithful. What if she *did* lose and Dad found out?

'Josh, I think ...' Betsey began.

'You're not changing your mind, are you? You're not turning chicken?' Josh called out. 'Cluck! Clu-uu-ck! Chicken!'

'No, I'm not. I'm ready when you are,' said Betsey. But as she spoke she was careful not to look at May. That didn't mean that she couldn't hear May tutting beside her though.

Josh walked to his starting position which was at the end of the path that led to the beach. Everyone followed him. May pulled Betsey back from the crowd.

'Betsey, you're making a big mistake.' May shook her head.

'Botheration, May! You're not my gran'ma. Don't you try to boss my head,' said Betsey annoyed.

'Are you really going to let Josh take all your marbles?' asked May. 'Even the one your dad gave you?'

'I'm going to win Josh's mighty marble,' Betsey said stubbornly. 'So Josh won't get any of my marbles. I won't lose a single one of them.'

'You've lost your marbles already if you think your itsy-bitsy bit of glass stands a chance against Josh's mighty marble,' said May.

Betsey began to feel bad. Worse than bad. Betsey began to feel terrible. She wished she'd never challenged Josh to this stupid contest.

'Come on then Betsey,' Josh called out. 'I'm bursting to win a whole bag of marbles.'

Betsey and May walked over to join Josh and the others.

'Josh, we can still have our contest but I don't want to include Old Faithful and ...'

But Josh didn't let Betsey finish.

'Cluck! Clu-uu-ck! Chicken!' Josh

began to leap about and peck and flap and strut, just like a chicken. 'Cluck! Clu-uu-ck!' Soon everyone else was doing the same thing. 'Clu-uu-ck!'

'Botheration!' said Betsey. 'Josh, you're about to lose Mr Mighty Marble.'

Betsey dug into her bag.

'What are you doing?' Josh frowned.

'Getting out a marble to play with,' answered Betsey.

'You've got to use Old Faithful,' Josh said. 'That was the deal.'

'But that's not fair. Your mighty marble is ginormous and Old Faithful is tiddly,' said Betsey.

'Too bad. That's the deal,'

smiled Josh.

What could Betsey do? The contest was all her idea so she couldn't back out now. There was nothing left to do but to stay put and play. Betsey felt her eyes stinging but she forced herself not to cry. She was going to lose all her precious marbles. All the marbles it had taken her so long to collect. And worse still, she was going to lose Old Faithful.

'Josh, you go first,' sniffed Betsey.

And the contest began. Everyone gathered round to watch. Josh flicked Mr Mighty Marble first. Betsey flicked Old Faithful away from Mr Mighty Marble. Josh flicked his marble towards Betsey's.

'Ooooh!' A gasp came from everyone around. Josh had only just missed Betsey's marble.

This was it. If Betsey didn't do something, Josh would hit her marble with his very next shot and then Betsey would lose every single marble she had in the world.

'Bombsies!' Betsey said.

Josh laughed. 'Bombsies! With that little marble! You can't win, Betsey, so give up now.'

'I'll show you,' Betsey said. She stood up, Old Faithful in her hand. She stood over Josh's marble carefully lining up Old Faithful over Mr Mighty Marble. If she missed, Josh would win for sure. No one spoke. The only sound came from the waves lapping on the white sand and the sound of birds singing from the trees.

'Your hand can't be lower than your waist,' Josh said.

'I know.' Betsey didn't look up. She carried on lining up her shot until Old Faithful was directly above Mr Mighty Marble. Then Betsey let go of her own marble. Old Faithful hit Mr Mighty Marble with a

CRR-AAA-CK!

Then a strange thing happened. Old Faithful bounced off Mr Mighty Marble.

'Ooooh!' said everyone.

Josh's marble wasn't well. It wasn't well at all. Mr Mighty Marble, Mr Super Mighty Marble, Mr Bigger-than-anyone-else's Marble had cracked into four pieces. Each piece lay on the path, glistening and glittering just as loudly as before.

Betsey picked up Old Faithful and stared at it.

'Wow, Betsey. That's some marble,' everyone said.

Josh carefully picked up the pieces that made up what used to be Mr Mighty Marble.

'Look what

you did.' Josh stared down at the pieces in his hand.

'Mr Mighty Marble doesn't look so mighty any more,' May laughed.

'Sorry, Josh,' Betsey said, 'You can have any five of my marbles if you want.' Betsey held out her bag of marbles.

'Can I have Old Faithful?' Josh asked hopefully.

'No chance!' said Betsey firmly. 'Old Faithful may be small, but he's a real super marble.'

Josh looked down and kicked at the ground with the toe of his right shoe.

'Come on, Josh,' smiled Betsey. 'I'll give you my second best marble instead.'

'Oh, all right then,' Josh said at last. Betsey handed over the bag and let Josh pick out five marbles he wanted.

Then Betsey, May and all their friends set off for home, telling tales of Old Faithful, the mightiest marble of them all.

6

Betsey Biggalow, the Detective

Betsey put down her book. So that's how Sam, the girl detective, found the missing money!

That was a good story, thought Betsey.

'Slinky, that was a good story.' Betsey picked up a book to show to her teddy bear.

But Slinky wasn't there ... Botheration! Where was Slinky Malinky?

Betsey searched here and there and everywhere, but she just couldn't find her. Slinky Malinky was a small orange teddy bear with a lop-sided smile and round, button eyes. Betsey didn't play with her teddy any more, but Slinky Malinky sat at the bottom of the bed and sometimes Betsey would talk to him. She'd had Slinky Malinky for a long time – ever since she could remember. Only now Slinky was *missing*. Where was she?

'There's only one thing for it,' Betsey muttered to herself. 'I'm going to have to become a detective, just like in my book, until I find her!'

Betsey had a long, hard think. Then she went into Mam and Dad's room and got one of Dad's old hats out of the wardrobe. The hat was far too big for her, so she had to tilt it well back off her forehead. She borrowed Mam's raincoat as well. It trailed along the floor so she had to hitch it up with the belt. Next she got one of Sherena's old notebooks and a pencil.

But there was still something missing.

Betsey wandered into Gran'ma Liz's room. And there she saw them – Gran'ma's spare pair of glasses! Betsey put them on and tried to look through them but she couldn't see a thing – everything was all blurred. She pushed the glasses down until they were perched on the end of her nose. Now she could look over them. Betsey looked at herself in the mirror. Perfect! She was all set. Now she looked just like a detective! She looked just like a real detective in one of those old films Gran'ma Liz liked so much. Betsey ran back to her bedroom.

Clues. The first thing to do was to search for clues. Here was one! Betsey found Slinky's red ribbon under the window. It should have been tied in a bow around teddy's neck ...

'What next!' Betsey wondered. And off she went to the sitting-room.

'Good grief, Betsey. What are you supposed to be?' asked Gran'ma Liz, looking up from her book.

'I'm a detective like in the old detective films,' said Betsey.

'Are those my spare pair of glasses?' Gran'ma Liz frowned.

Betsey nodded. 'I'll be very careful with them Gran'ma Liz – honest,' she said quickly.

'Hhmm! Well, just make sure you are,' said Gran'ma Liz. 'So what can I do for you Detective Biggalow?'

'I'd like to ask you a few questions,' said Betsey.

'Go on then,' Gran'ma liz smiled.

'Gran'ma, when was the last time you saw Slinky Malinky?' asked Betsey.

'Hhmm! Well now ... let me see ...' Gran'ma Liz lowered her book and pondered. 'It was ... it must have been three nights ago when your mam was working late. I tucked you in and read you a story – remember? Wasn't Slinky Malinky at the bottom of your bed then?'

Betsey wrote down 'GRAN'MA

LIZ' in her book and underlined it three times. Under that she wrote, 'Three nights ago on my bed.'

'Thanks Gran'ma Liz,' said Betsey. And off she went to find her bigger brother. Desmond was in the back yard, bowling a cricket ball to his friend Sam. Betsey went and stood right in between them.

'Desmond, when was the last time you saw Slinky Malinky?' Betsey asked.

'Your teddy bear?' Desmond frowned.

'That's right,' replied Betsey.

'I haven't a clue when I last saw Slinky,' Desmond said.

Betsey wrote down 'DESMOND'

in her notebook and underlined it three times.

'Desmond, how do you spell "unhelpful"?' Betsey asked.

Desmond told her. Betsey wrote UNHELPFUL in great big capital letters under his name.

'Why have you got on Dad's hat and Mam's old coat?' Desmond asked.

'Because I'm Betsey Biggalow, The Great Detective, and detectives always wear raincoats and hats,' answered Betsey.

'Your sister is a nut!' Sam said to Desmond.

Desmond shook his head. 'I know. I hope it's not catching!'

Betsey ignored them and rushed off. She didn't feel any closer to finding Slinky Malinky. Betsey ran to see her bigger sister. Sherena was doing her homework.

'Sherena, when was the last time you saw Slinky malinky?' Betsey asked.

'Who are you supposed to be?' Sherena laughed.

'I'm a detective. And I should be asking the questions, not you,' said Betsey.

Sherena raised her eyebrows. 'Excuse me!'

'Well, when was

the last time you saw Slinky Malinky?' Betsey repeated.

'Yesterday,' Sherena remembered. 'She was on my bed, so I threw her back onto yours.'

'Hhmm!' Betsey wrote 'SHERENA' in her notepad and underlined it three times. Under that she wrote – 'Yesterday on her bed.' But that gave Betsey an idea.

Betsey went back into her bedroom. She took off her hat and walked over to Sherena's bed. Where would Slinky have landed when Sherena threw her across the room? Betsey folded up her dad's hat until it was Slinky-sized. Then she squatted on Sherena's bed until she was

Sherena's height and threw the hat across the room. The hat bounced off Betsey's bed and landed behind it. Betsey raced across the room. This had to be it! Slinky must be behind the bed.

Betsey pulled her bed further away from the wall and ... how strange! Slinky wasn't there, but some of Slinky's stuffing was. Betsey recognised it at once. And next to the stuffing were some longish, dark brown hairs ... The hairs looked strangely familiar ...

Betsey put her dad's hat back on and picked up her two new clues. The stuffing she put in her coat pocket, but she held on to the hairs.

‘I bet these belong to the person who kidnapped Slinky,’ said Betsey.

She went into the sitting-room and checked them against Gran’ma Liz’s hair. Gran’ma’s hair was longish, but grey not brown. Betsey held up her newest clue to Sherena’s head, but Sherena’s hair was jet black and long. Betsey compared the hairs she’d found to Desmond’s hair but Desmond’s hair was shorter and curlier. Betsey even tried matching the hairs she’d found against Sam’s head, but they didn’t match either. Sam had even less hair than Desmond!

Betsey sat down on a kitchen chair with her head in her hands. Botheration! Now what should she do?

She'd asked Gran'ma Liz and Desmond and Sherena about Slinky Malinky and none of them knew where her teddy was. Mam was at work so there was no one else to ask – unless you included Prince, the Alsatian dog. Prince was there, lying under the window.

'It's a pity you can't talk to me, Prince,' sighed Betsey. ' Maybe then you could tell me when you last saw my teddy bear.'

'Wooof!' barked Prince, and out he ran into the back yard. Betsey looked down at the hairs in her hand, then out of the kitchen window at Prince, then back down at the hairs.

'Got it! I know who did it!' exclaimed Betsey. She dashed out into the yard. Sam and Desmond were still playing cricket. Prince was at the back of the yard digging furiously.

'Desmond! Sam! Quick! It's Prince. Prince kidnapped Slinky Malinky!' Betsey shouted, chasing down the yard after Prince.

'How do you know that?' frowned Desmond.

'I found some of Prince's hairs in my bedroom, along with some of Slinky's stuffing. I'm sure it's Prince,' said Betsey. 'Prince, you bad dog, what have you done with my teddy bear?'

'**Woooo-oooooof!**' barked Prince, digging even more furiously than before.

At that very second, Prince raised his head, his tail wagging faster than fast. And what did he have in his mouth? Slinky Malinky! A very dirty, dusty Slinky Malinky who was a lot skinnier than the last time Betsey saw her!

'Prince, you ought to be ashamed,' said Betsey. '*You're* the kidnapper!' I *knew* these dark brown hairs belonged to you! I'm not going to pat you for finding my teddy when you buried her in the first place!'

Betsey took her teddy away from Prince. Slinky Malinky was filthy. 'I'll have to get Mam to wash her now,' frowned Betsey.

'And look what else is in here.' Desmond pointed to the hole in that Prince had dug. 'That's Mam's tape measure ... and Gran'ma Liz's perfume bottle ...'

'Desmond, isn't that your school book?' asked Sam.

'Yes it is!' said Desmond, surprised. 'My teacher told me off because I couldn't find it. Prince, you bad dog!'

'I told you I was a great detective,' said Betsey. 'Not only did I rescue Slinky Malinky, but I found things I didn't even know I was looking for in the first place!'

7

Betsey and the Insult Contest

Betsey came home from school, with her chin drooping and her mouth frowning and tears in her eyes.

'Betsey child, what's the matter with you?' asked Gran'ma Liz, immediately concerned.

'I ... I had a quarrel with May,'

Betsey whispered.

'A quarrel? What about?' asked Gran'ma.

Betsey didn't answer. She just shook her head and stared down at her sandals.

That evening, Betsey hardly touched her dinner. It was one of her favourites too – flying fish and french fries and fresh salad. There was a huge jug of orange juice in the middle of the table but Betsey didn't ask for seconds and thirds the way she usually did. She drank half a glass of orange juice and left the rest. Gran'ma Liz and Sherena and Desmond looked at each other, then at Betsey. They were beginning to get worried.

After dinner Betsey moped around the house, sighing and sniffing and not saying a word, until Desmond and Sherena couldn't stand it any more.

'Betsey, what did you and May have an argument about?' asked Sherena.

'Nothing much,' Betsey replied.

'Go on. You can tell us. Why did you and May have a bust up?' Desmond asked.

'I'm not telling you,' sniffed Betsey.

'Come on, Betsey. We want to help,' said Sherena.

'Yeah! I miss having you bouncing around the house and

chatting so much I can't hear myself think,' said Desmond.

'So why did you and May fall out? said Gran'ma Liz.

'It doesn't matter,' sighed Betsey. And off she walked.

At last Mam came home, but Betsey wouldn't even tell Mam what was wrong. She just wandered around the house, her face as long as a tree trunk, saying, 'It doesn't matter. It doesn't matter..

'Mam, do something,' Sherena whispered, when Betsey couldn't hear.

'She's driving us nuts!' said Desmond. 'I thought Betsey was bad enough when she made a lot of noise, but she's even worse when she's quiet!'

'All right, then,' said Mam. 'Let me phone up May's mam. Maybe May told her what's going on.'

So Mam phoned May's house and was on the phone for quite a while. When at last she put the phone down, Mam had a deep frown on her face.

'Well? What's going on?' asked Gran'ma Liz.

'May won't tell her mam what they quarrelled about either,' said Mam. 'I think it's time for me to take the matter into my own hands.'

'What d'you mean, Mam?' asked Desmond.

'You'll see.' That's all Mam would say.

The next day was a Saturday. A beautiful, sunny Saturday with not a cloud in the sky. Not that Betsey noticed. She moped around the house quieter than a mouse.

'Betsey, do you want to ride my bike?' Sherena asked.

'No, thank you,' said Betsey, her head bent.

Sherena

stared at her in amazement. Betsey had never before said no to riding Sherena's bike. Usually Betsey pouted and pestered and badgered and bothered Sherena for a ride, until Sherena usually gave in, to get some peace.

Betsey wandered out into the back yard.

'Betsey, let's make a bow and some arrows. We could have an archery contest,' said Desmond.

'No, thank you,' Betsey sighed.

Desmond stared at her in disbelief. Betsey had been asking him to show her how to make a bow and arrow from tree branches for the last month. And now, he'd offered to show her and she'd turned him down flat. Desmond watched as Betsey wandered back into the house.

Later that afternoon, Sherena whispered to Desmond, 'Is Betsey back to normal yet?'

'No. And I offered to make a bow and arrow with her,' said Desmond.

'I offered her a ride on my bike and she said no,' said Sherena.

'This is serious,' said Desmond.

And off they went to find Mam.

'Mam, we're worried about Betsey,' said Sherena.

Just at that moment, the front door opened.

'We're here!' called out May's mam.

Mam, Sherena and Desmond

went into the sitting-room. May and her mam were standing there. May and Betsey stood facing each other but neither of them said a word.

'Betsey, say hello to May then,' said Mam.

Betsey didn't say a word.

'May, say hello to your friend Betsey,' said May's mam.

May turned her head away.

'It was the same thing last night,' said May's mam. 'May moped around the house and she hardly touched her dinner, but she wouldn't tell me what she and Betsey had argued about.'

All right then,' Betsey's mam said firmly. 'Betsey sit here. May, you sit down next to her.'

Betsey sat down on the sofa and May sat down next to her, although they were careful not to touch each other.

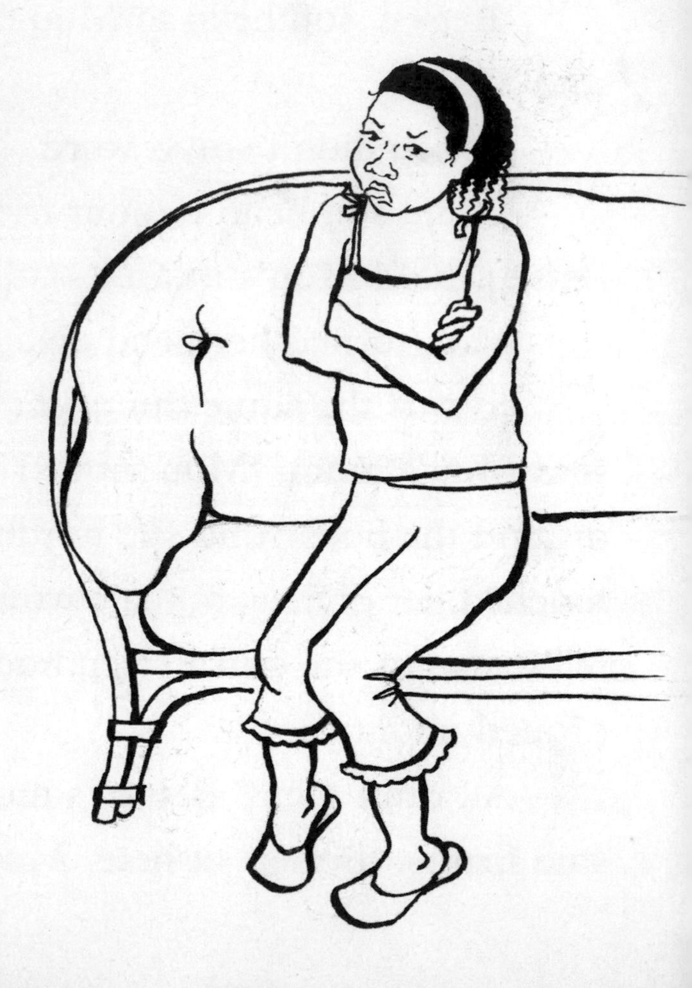

'Right then, you two,' said Mam. 'You're going to have an insult contest.'

'An insult contest?' said Betsey, surprised, 'What's that?'

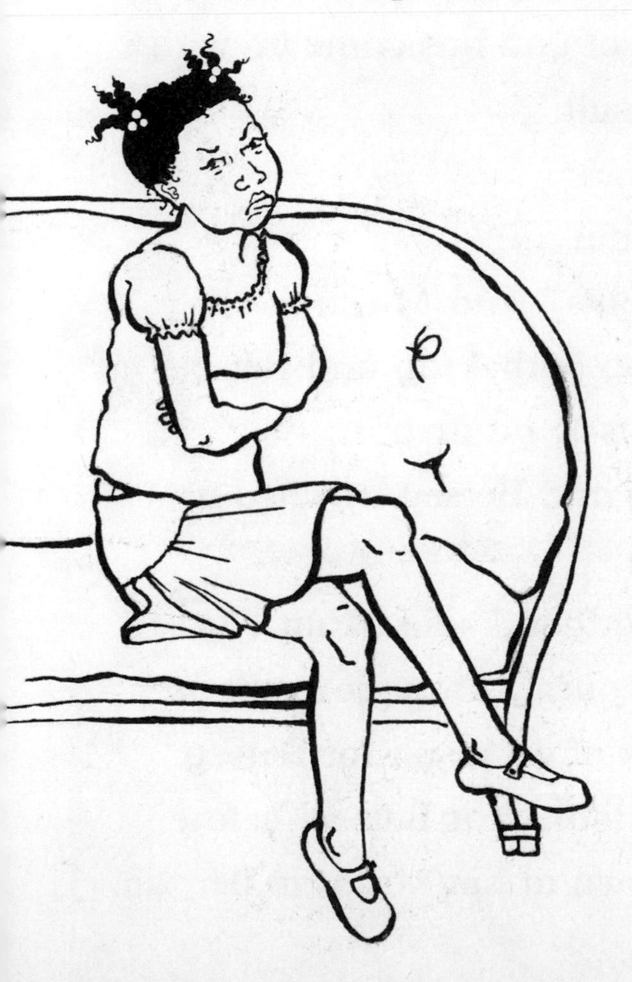

'Both of you will take it in turns to insult each other. The rest of us are going to sit opposite you and watch and listen. At the end of it we'll judge which one of you has come up with the best insult.'

'But ...'

'Oh, but ...'

'No buts,' said Mam, interrupting both May and Betsey. 'Who wants to go first?'

'May and Betsey frowned at each other.

'Okay then,' said Mam. 'As you're the guest, May. you can go first. Think of an insult for Betsey.'

May looked at Betsey, before looking down at her hands in her lap.

She muttered something under her breath.

'We didn't quite catch that, May,' said Mam. 'Please say it again.'

'I said that Betsey is a cabbage head,' said May, very loudly this time.

'A cabbage head? Well your head is shaped just like a dog biscuit and your ears are tiny like raisins!' said Betsey annoyed.

'So my head's like a dog biscuit, is it? Well, you're a ... a ... slimy snake ...' began May.

'Ah! Can't allow that one,' Mam interrupted. 'Snakes aren't slimy. Their skin is quite dry.'

Mam turned to May's mam and

Sherena and Desmond. 'Do you all agree? she asked.

They all nodded.

'May, you'll have to come up with another insult,' said Mam.

'Betsey is a toad face ...' said May.

'You're a smelly sock ...' said Betsey.

'You're a stinky sock ...'

'You're more stinky than me ...'

'No, I'm not ...'

Yes, you are ...'

'You're a tissue that someone's blown their nose into lots and lots of times ...' said May.

'You're the inside of Desmond's sweaty, smelly sports bag when he's been playing cricket,' said Betsey.

Something very strange was happening. May's lips quivered and Betsey's lips twitched with each new insult that they flung at each other.

'Well, you're a ... a ...' May began.

'And you're a ... you're a ...' Betsey started.

But neither of them finished their insults. They both began to giggle, then to chuckle, then to roar with laughter. Which was just as well, because Betsey's mam and May's mam and Sherena

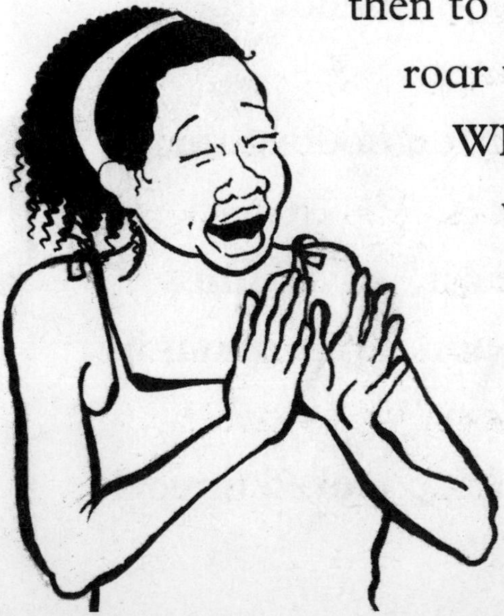

and Desmond were
all laughing so hard
that they wouldn't
have heard the
next lot of
insults anyway.

'I'm sorry, Betsey,' smiled May.

'I'm sorry too,' Betsey smiled back.

'So are you two friends again?' asked Mam.

Betsey and May nodded their heads.

'Glad to hear it,' said May's mam. 'What did you argue about in the first place?'

Betsey and May looked at each

other, surprised.

'I can't remember,' said Betsey.

'Neither can I!' said May.

'Never mind,' said Betsey. 'Let's go and play down by the beach.'

'You bet!' said May.

Betsey and May bounced off the sofa and ran for the front door.

'Before you disappear, Betsey,' said Desmond, calling after his sister, 'I just want to say one thing.'

'What's that?' asked Betsey.

'The inside of my sports bag is not sweaty and smelly!' said Desmond.

'Desmond, go and stick your nose in it and then say that,' said Mam. 'Betsey described your sports bag perfectly!'

Get Lost, Betsey!

Betsey hopped from foot to foot as if her toes were on fire. Today was going to be an excellent day! Betsey and her family were all going to the market – and oh, how Betsey loved the market! But there was an extra special reason why Betsey was so excited.

'Dad's coming home soon!' Betsey beamed.

'Not until next week, Betsey,' Sherena reminded her.

'But next week is sooner rather than later,' Betsey pointed out.

Dad was abroad studying to be a doctor and it'd been ages since Betsey had last seen him. Although he sent lots of letters and phoned every weekend, it just wasn't the same.

But at last he was coming home.

That's why Betsey's whole family were going to market, to get in all of Dad's favourite foods and to buy other provisions to make him feel really welcome.

'Hurry up, Sherena. You're too

slow! If we wait for you, we'll never get to town.' Betsey ran over to Sherena and started tugging up the zip at the back of her dress.

'OUCH!' Sherena yelled. 'Betsey, you're supposed to zip up the dress, not my skin!'

'I'm only trying to help,' said Betsey.

'Then get lost and leave me to do it,' said Sherena. 'You're kind of help is too painful!'

Betsey raced into Desmond's room.

'Desmond! You're not ready. Hurry up!' said Betsey.

'I just need to put my shoes on,' said Desmond.

'I'll get them for you,' Betsey offered.

Betsey saw Desmond's shoes under his bed and ran past him to get them.

'OW! Betsey, those are my toes, not the carpet,' Desmond yelled as Betsey trod on his foot!

'It's okay, you've got five more on that foot!' said Betsey, pointing to the foot she *hadn't* stepped on.

'That's not funny!' fumed Desmond.

'Don't be so grouchy, potato head!' said Betsey.

'I'll stop being a grouch if you go away, get lost, close the door on your way out, put an egg in your shoe and beat it, make like a tree and leave!' Desmond said.

'All right! I'll go. But I don't care what you say to me today, because we're going to town. *And Dad's coming home soon!*' Betsey smiled.

Betsey darted out of the room.

SMACK! She crashed straight into Sherena. And was Sherena pleased? No, she wasn't.

'Betsey, why don't you watch where you're going?' snapped Sherena.

'She's a real pest, isn't she?' Desmond agreed.

'That's quite enough from both of you.' Gran'ma Liz appeared from nowhere and glared at Sherena and Desmond. 'You two say sorry to your sister.'

'Sorry, Betsey,' Sherena and Desmond said at once.

They'd both seen that look on Gran'ma Liz's face before and they weren't about to argue!

'Now let's get going!' smiled Gran'ma Liz.

And at last they were off.

When they got off the bus in town, Betsey hardly knew where to look first. All different kinds of fish and flowers and food and fruit filled the market stalls. Paw-paws, mangoes, bananas, cherries, sugar apples and coconuts on some stalls. Swordfish, flying fish, red mullet and salt fish on others. Sweet potatoes, yams, breadfruits, green bananas, eddoes and okras on still more. Betsey didn't even want to blink in case she missed something.

'Gran'ma Liz! Isn't it extra-amazing?' asked Betsey, her eyes wider than wide.

'Yes, child,' smiled Gran'ma Liz. 'And tiring! And noisy!'

Betsey and her family weaved their way through the masses of people, looking at stall after stall.

'Betsey, stay close to me. I don't want you wandering off,' said Gran'ma Liz.

'No, Gran'ma.'

'Mam, I'm just going to do some window shopping,' said Sherena.

'I think I'll join you,' said Desmond.

'Can I come? Let me come!' said Betsey.

'No way!' Desmond and Sherena said at once.

Gran'ma Liz looked at Sherena and Desmond. 'You two aren't being very kind to your sister today.' Betsey, go along with them, but don't give them any trouble.

Betsey grinned up at Desmond and Sherena. She was happy about going with them, even if they weren't.

'I'll meet you three at Joe's ice-cream stand in an hour,' said Mam, glancing down at her watch.

'Come on then, Betsey,' tutted Sherena.

And off Desmond and Sherena marched. Betsey had to trot to keep up with them but she didn't mind. It was better than being with the grown-ups!

'Keep up with us, Betsey,' said Desmond. 'We don't want you slowing us down.'

'Don't worry,' said Betsey.

On the very next stall there were coconut cakes, all kind of doughnuts, fresh biscuits and her favourite – banana fritters! They all smelt so scrumptious. Betsey stopped and breathed deeply to get the full effect.

'Look at these!' Betsey called out to her brother and sister who were now some way ahead of her.

'Betsey, get a move on,' Sherena called back before she carried on walking.

Betsey ran to catch up with them – and then she saw it! A toy stall! There were rows and rows of rag dolls, bean bags, playing cards, bouncing balls and ... *marbles.*

Betsey had never seen so many marbles. Hundreds and hundreds of them piled up in buckets. Big ones, little ones, bright ones, glittering ones, marbles that were all one colour and marbles where all the colours fought for space to shine.

'D'you like my marbles?' smiled

the woman on the stall.

'Oh yes!' breathed Betsey. 'They're beautiful.'

'Bring your mam along and I'll sell you some,' said the woman.

Mam! Betsey looked around quickly. Where were Sherena and Desmond? Where were Mam and Gran'ma Liz? She couldn't see any of them.

Betsey jumped up and down, trying to see over the heads of all the grown-ups around her, but they were too tall. Betsey's heart suddenly began to hammer in her chest. She raced forward, looking for Desmond and Sherena.

They were nowhere to be found.

Betsey ran past stall after stall but ... nothing. She turned around but she didn't see anything or anyone she recognised.

'Botheration!' said Betsey. 'Botheration! Botheration!' She said it two more times!

'I'll go back and try to find Mam and Gran'ma Liz,' Betsey decided.

Betsey headed back the way she'd come but that didn't do any good either. There was noise and bustle and fuss everywhere Betsey turned. The market wasn't a wonderful place any more. It was big and noisy and frightening. Betsey began to sniff. Her eyes started to sting with tears.

'If you cry, you won't see anything at all,' Betsey muttered sternly to herself.

But it didn't help.

All Betsey wanted to do now was find Mam and go home.

'Hello, sugar. Did you find your Mam? Are you going to buy some of my marbles?'

Betsey turned her head. She was in front of the toy stall again.

The woman behind the stall smiled at Betsey – and that was it. Betsey burst into tears!

'What's the matter?' Immediately the woman came out from behind her stall and squatted down in front of Betsey. 'Are you all right?'

'I can't find my mam,' Betsey wiped her eyes.

'Hhmm!' said the woman. 'I think the best thing to do is find a policeman. D'you agree?'

Betsey nodded. The stall woman stood up and looked around.

'There's one. OFFICER!'

A policeman came over to the toy stall.

'What's the problem?' asked the

policeman, smiling kindly at Betsey.

'I can't find my mam,' said Betsey.

'Where d'you live?' asked the policeman.

Betsey had just opened her mouth to tell him when, 'BETSEY!'

And Betsey was swept off her feet and hugged so tightly by her mam that she could hardly breathe. Betsey looked around. Sherena, Desmond and Gran'ma Liz were all trying to hug her too!

'Elizabeth Ruby Biggalow! You had us all worried sick,' said Gran'ma Liz.

'I know this morning, we told you to get lost ...' began Sherena.

'But we didn't mean it,' finished Desmond.

'Sherena and Desmond, the next time you take your sister somewhere with you, don't wander off and leave her to get lost,' said Mam firmly.

'I wasn't lost. I knew exactly where I was,' said Betsey. 'I was in the market, looking for all of you. That means you were the ones who were lost, not me!'

'Betsey,' Sherena shook her head as everyone else laughed. 'I wonder about you sometimes. I really do!'

Betsey Flies a Kite

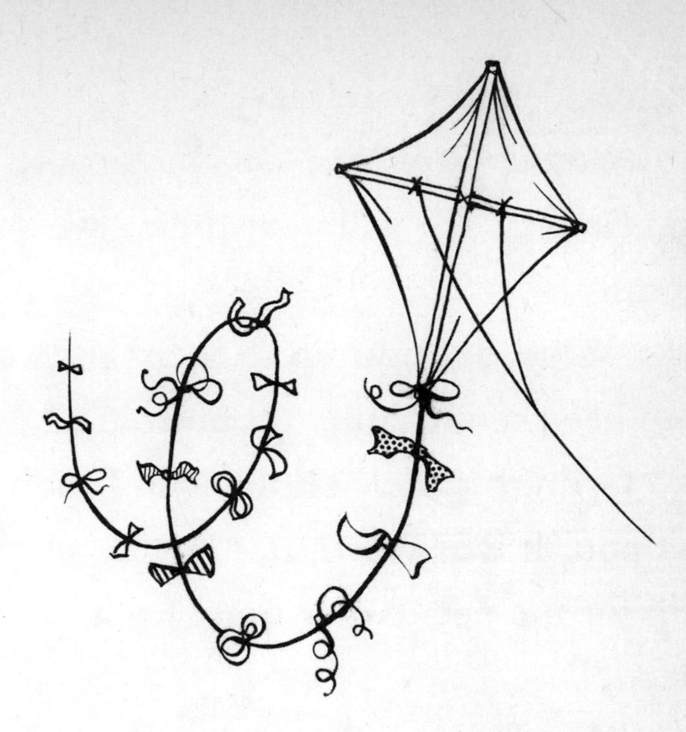

Gran'ma Liz was busy hanging out the clothes on the washing line. Desmond and Betsey were sitting at the bottom of the garden, their heads bent over something.

'Desmond, Betsey, I thought you two were going to help me with the washing,' said Gran'ma Liz.

'Sorry, Gran'ma Liz. We forgot,' said Betsey. 'We will next time – we promise.'

'What are you up to then? You've both been really quiet all morning,' said Gran'ma Liz. 'That's why I didn't call you. It was worth not having your help for the peace and quiet I got instead!'

'I'm showing Betsey how to make something,' said Desmond.

'Hhmm! Well, whatever you do, mind the clothes. I've only just washed them and they're not dry yet,' Gran'ma Liz said.

'We won't go anywhere near the clothes, Gran'ma – honest!' said Betsey.

'Hhmm! Just make sure we've got everything we need,' said Desmond. 'Have we got string?'

'We've got a huge ball of string. Here it is,' replied Betsey.

'Just say "check", Betsey or we'll be here all day,' smiled Desmond. 'Now then, we need two long branches, one slightly longer than the other.'

'Got them. Check!' said Betsey.

'Strong, coloured tissue paper?'

'Check!'

'Sticky tape?'

'Check!'

'Some old pieces of ribbon?' Desmond asked.

'I got these from Mam. Check!' answered Betsey.

'Scissors?'

'Check!'

'Then we're all set,' said Desmond.

'Hooray!' shouted Betsey. 'We're going to make a kite!'

Desmond grinned. 'The first thing to do is to make a cross using the branches. Then tie them together using some string.'

'Check!' said Betsey. And she picked up the branches and laid the shorter one over the longer one. The she got some string and tied the two branches together so that they formed a cross shape.

'Make sure you tie the string good and tight,' said Desmond.

Betsey tied it very slowly and carefully, wrapping it round the branches, first one way, then the other. Then she tied the two ends of string in a tight knot.

'That's good,' Desmond said. 'Now we have to spread out the tissue paper and place the branches on it.'

'Like this?' Betsey asked.

'That's right,' replied Desmond.

For the next hour Desmond and Betsey worked at making the kite. They cut two large diamond shapes out of the flaming-red tissue paper and stuck them to the branches. They tied tiny bits of ribbon to a piece of string as long as Betsey's arm and then tied that on to the bottom of the kite. Then they attached one end of the ball of string to the bottom of the kite as well.

At last Desmond and Betsey jumped up! They had finished! They were ready to try it out. Betsey hopped up and down. She'd done it! She'd made her very first kite!

'Woof!' Prince, the Alsatian dog, tried to sniff around the kite as Betsey held it up.

'No, Prince. Bad dog! That kite isn't for you,' said Desmond.

'Where are we going to fly it?' Betsey asked excitedly.

'We can practise a few things here,' Desmond decided. 'Then we'll go to the beach and fly it really high.'

'Will it swoop and soar and glide?' asked Betsey, her eyes wide.

'Of course it will,' laughed Desmond. 'We built it!'

'So what should we practise first?'

Betsey asked.

'The run up,' said Desmond. 'Betsey, you stand here and hold the kite in your hands. Then run to the other end of the yard, letting the kite go at the same time. You've also got to let the string out as you run so that the kite has a chance to rise into the air. Have you got all that?'

It was a lot to remember all at once, but Betsey knew she could do it.

This is going to be easy, Betsey thought.

The only trouble was, as soon as she started running, Prince started chasing behind her.

'Wooof! Wooof!' barked Prince. He wanted to be part of the game too.

'Botheration, Prince! I'll never get this right if you don't behave yourself,' said Betsey, crossly.

Betsey ran to the back of the yard to try again.

'Woooooof!' Prince chased behind her, trying to leap up at the kite.

'Desmond!' Betsey pleaded.

Desmond held Prince's collar while Betsey did her run. The kite barely lifted higher than her waist before it collapsed to the ground.

'Run faster, Betsey,' Desmond suggested. 'And hold the kite up higher before you let it go.'

'Check!' said Betsey, walking back to one end of the yard.

'Ready? GO!' shouted Desmond.

And off Betsey ran. She released the kite so that she was only holding on to it by its string and ran even faster. The kite flapped and fluttered, but it began to *rise*.

'Yippee! It's working! It's working,' shouted Betsey.

'Yeah! Go Betsey! Go!' Desmond jumped up and down.

But then it happened ... The kite got caught up in the washing line. Desmond was so busy jumping up and down that he forgot to hold onto Prince's collar. Prince raced across the yard and started jumping up at the kite, barking madly.

'No, Prince. **DON'T ...**' squeaked Betsey.

She grabbed for Prince. Prince grabbed for the kite and … the whole washing line came tumbling down.

Oh no! Desmond and Betsey and Prince stared at the shirts and socks and underclothes and dresses and trousers all over the ground.

'We're in trouble now …' Desmond sighed.

Sure enough, in about two seconds flat, Gran'ma Liz came storming out of the house.

'Desmond, Betsey, I thought I told you two to mind the washing,' fumed Gran'ma Liz.

'But Gran'ma Liz, Prince …' Betsey began.

'It was Prince who …' Desmond tried.

'Not another word.' Gran'ma Liz interrupted them both. 'You two are going to help me wash every single one of these things again.'

'Oh, but we wanted to fly our kite,' said Betsey.

'Not a chance! Not until all the washing has been redone. And you can start by gathering it all up again,' said Gran'ma Liz, and she marched back into the house.

Betsey and Desmond turned to Prince. Prince watched them, his tail between his legs, his head hanging down.

'Botheration, Prince!' said Betsey, crossly. 'Double and triple botheration!'

'Woof!' Prince apologised.

'Well, you did promise Gran'ma that we'd help her next time she did the washing,' Desmond reminded his sister.

'Yes,' replied Betsey, 'but I didn't think we'd be helping Gran'ma quite so soon!'

10
Magic
Betsey

'Ladies and gentlemen, Betsey the great, Betsey the wonderful, Betsey the magnificent will now put on a magic show for you! A magic show so excellent that nothing like it has ever been seen before and will never be seen again.'

'Betsey, get on with it,' Desmond said.

Betsey ignored him! She wasn't Betsey Biggalow, Desmond's sister any more. Oh no! She was Betsey the magician! Betsey's Uncle George had bought her a book on magic tricks and Betsey had spent the last few days reading it and practising her tricks over and over. And now she was ready.

Betsey looked down at the table which had all the things she needed for her magic tricks on it.

'What shall I do first?' Betsey wondered out loud.

'Today, Betsey! Today!' said Sherena. 'I've got other things to do, you know.'

'Botheration, Sherena. You can't rush real magic!' Betsey said. Being a magician was hard work!

'Mam, can I leave?' Sherena asked.

'No!' said Mam firmly. And that was the end of that!

'Okay then,' said Betsey. 'Before I do anything else, I have to wave my magic wand over this table or none of my tricks will work.'

Betsey picked up her wand. She'd made it by covering a twig from the garden with some tinfoil and it looked perfect! She waved it over the table and said the magic words, 'Betsey magic! Magic Betsey! Do your magic!

Show us! Let's see!'

'Oh, good grief!' said Desmond.

Gran'ma Liz gave him one of her looks and he shut up!

'For my first trick, I'm going to ask Sherena to pick a card,' said Betsey.

She walked over to Sherena and fanned out the cards in front of her, face down.

'Pick a card then,' Betsey urged.

Sherena picked out a card and looked at it.

'Now put it back,' said Betsey.

Carefully, Sherena put the card back into the middle of the pile. Betsey split the pile of cards into two and turned to walk back to the table. She knew Sherena's card was on top of the pile in her left hand. She picked it up and stuffed it up her shirt sleeve, keeping it in place by squeezing her arm against her side. It was difficult – especially as her sleeves were short! Then Betsey turned around to face her audience.

'I will now shuffle the cards and produce Sherena's card by magic!' said Betsey.

'And some cheating while your back was turned,' muttered Desmond.

'I don't need to cheat. I'm a real magician,' Betsey said loftily. She shuffled the cards. tapped them with her wand, then shuffled them again. But this time she quickly tried to reach

up and fish the card out of her sleeve
at the same time. It
didn't work. The
cards flew
into the air.

'BETSEY! Those are my cards you're bending and ruining,' said Sherena.

'Botheration, Sherena. I'm not ruining your cards. They're ruining my trick!' said Betsey.

Mam and Gran'ma Liz just looked at each other. Betsey bent down to pick up the cards that now lay scattered at her feet.

RIP! As Betsey tugged at the card beneath her left foot, half of it stayed under her foot and the other half was left in Betsey's hand.

'Betsey! I told you to be careful with my cards.' Sherena sprang off the sofa. 'Look what you've done!'

'Sorry, Sherena. It wasn't

purpose work,' Betsey said quickly.

'Is that it then?' asked Desmond, standing up. 'Can we go now?'

'But I haven't finished,' said Betsey.

Desmond sat down again. They all waited for Betsey to move on to her next trick.

'This next one is a water trick,' said Betsey. 'But first I have to say the magic words – "Betsey magic! Show us! Let's see!"'

Betsey picked up a glass off the table.

'I'm holding an ordinary glass of water in my right hand and an ordinary piece of card in my left hand,' said Betsey.

She walked over to Mam. 'I will now tip the glass upside down over Mam's head but the water will stay in the glass.'

'Er, do your trick over Desmond's head, please' said Mam.

'Over my head! No, thank you,' Desmond said quickly.

'This trick will work, Desmond. I promise,' Betsey pleaded.

'Oh, all right then,' Desmond grumbled. 'But I'd better not get wet, Betsey.'

Betsey carefully put the piece of card on top of the full glass and then turned them both upside down. She then stretched out her arms until the glass was directly over Desmond's head.

'I don't like this ...' Desmond said, hardly daring to blink.

'I will now take the card away and the water will stay in the glass,' announced Betsey confidently.

'Betsey ...'

'Trust me, Desmond,' Betsey whispered.

Slowly, she removed the card. To everyone's amazement the water stayed in the glass. Mam, Gran'ma Liz and Sherena all started clapping, really impressed. Betsey grinned.

'It's working?' Desmond couldn't believe it. He looked up and **WHOOSH**! Water came flooding out all over his face!

Gran'ma Liz, Sherena and Mam

all sprang off the sofa before they got drenched as well.

'Elizabeth Ruby Biggalow, just look what you've done to the sofa,' Mam said.

'The clingfilm came off the top of the glass,' Betsey wailed. 'It wasn't meant to do that!'

Desmond leapt up, coughing and spluttering. 'Look what you've done! I'm soaking wet!'

Mam, Sherena and Gran'ma Liz looked at him, flapping about like a fish out of water. They couldn't help it. They all burst out laughing!

'It's not funny,' Desmond said annoyed.

'Yes, it is,' Sherena grinned.

'Betsey, that's the first and last time I ever let you do your magic tricks anywhere near me,' said Desmond crossly.

'But I've got a string trick and a coin trick and a marble trick to do yet,' said Betsey.

'Betsey dear, I think it's time for you to call it a day,' said Gran'ma Liz.

Gran'ma Liz went into the kitchen to get a drink, followed by Mam and Sherena. Desmond went to his bedroom to change his clothes, giving Betsey a dirty look on his way out of the living-room.

Sadly, Betsey wandered out into the front yard. Everything had gone wrong, wrong, wrong. Then Betsey

spotted someone walking up the road who had her jumping up and down and gasping with excitement. She ran forward to meet him.

Five minutes later, Betsey ran into the house.

'Everyone! Everyone, where are you?' Betsey shouted.

Gran'ma Liz, Mam, Sherena and Desmond all came running.

'What's the matter, Betsey?'

'What's happened?'

'I've got another trick for you,'

said Betsey.

'Is that all?' frowned Sherena.

'Betsey, don't shout like that. I thought there was something wrong with you,' said Mam.

'Please! Just one more trick. It's my best trick ever and this time it *will* work. Guaranteed!' said Betsey excitedly.

'All right then. But this is the last one,' said Mam.

'You've all got to stand over there,' said Betsey. And she shooed her family over to the window.

Betsey walked back to the open living-room door and stood by it.

'And now, Betsey the tremendous, Betsey the stupendous

will make a real, live person appear before your very eyes,' said Betsey proudly. 'I'll just say the magic words first ...'

'Oh, not again,' said Sherena.

'I have to, or the trick won't work,' said Betsey. Then she began.

'Betsey magic!
Magic Betsey!
Do your magic!
Show us!
Let's see!'

Betsey waved her wand three times in the air and –

Dad sprang up from behind the sofa. 'Hi there!' he grinned.

'DAD!'

The whole family came running over.

'I told you I was magic!' said Betsey proudly.

'You saw Dad outside and got him to sneak behind the sofa for your trick, didn't you?' asked Desmond.

'No, she didn't,' said Dad, hugging everyone at once. 'Betsey waved her wand and here I am! She really is a magic Betsey!'

And with that Dad winked at Betsey – and Betsey winked back!

See you soon.

Betsey x